Jacqueline J. Vivelo
Reading to Matthew

ILLUSTRATED BY
Birgitta Saflund

Roberts Rinehart Publishers

TEXT COPYRIGHT © 1993 BY JACQUELINE J. VIVELO
ARTWORK COPYRIGHT © 1993 BY BIRGITTA SAFLUND

PUBLISHED IN THE UNITED STATES OF AMERICA
BY ROBERTS RINEHART PUBLISHERS
121 SECOND AVENUE, NIWOT, COLORADO 80544

PUBLISHED IN IRELAND AND GREAT BRITAIN
BY ROBERTS RINEHART PUBLISHERS
SCHULL, WEST CORK, REPUBLIC OF IRELAND

PUBLISHED IN CANADA BY
KEY PORTER BOOKS
70 THE ESPLANADE
TORONTO, ONTARIO M5E 1R2

ISBN 1-879373-60-2
LIBRARY OF CONGRESS CATALOG CARD NUMBER 93-84912

PRINTED AND BOUND IN HONG KONG BY COLORCORP

I was fourteen when my brother Matthew was knocked out one day at school. It was an accident that could have happened to anybody. But Matthew didn't regain consciousness. When they finally let me see him, he looked strange just lying there. I'd have tried anything I could think of to help, but a week passed before I thought of anything.

I couldn't seem to concentrate that week, not on school, not on television, not on books—especially not on books.

Matthew and I had been reading *The Call of the Wild* together; but, after I saw him and knew he couldn't listen any more, I lost interest. I couldn't bring myself to read it alone. You see, I've been reading to Matthew almost all his life.

My mom has a theory that you should start reading to kids as soon as they're born. She says she started reading to me before I left the hospital. I know for a fact that she was reading to the twins before they were a week old. When people try to tell her how dumb it is, she just waves her hand and says, "Look at my kids! They were all reading by the time they were four."

She also believes that kids can understand anything that someone takes the time to explain; "anything" includes cubism and the theory of relativity, as well as what's happening to water when it boils. I don't know how well her theories work, but they didn't seem to hurt me or the twins. The twins are my sisters Anne and Kate. When I was seven and they were five, Matthew was born.

Of course, Mom started him off just the way she did the rest of us. Then, when he was not quite two years old, she told us she was going back to work. She was glad about everything except Matthew. She said he would be well taken care of, but there wouldn't be as much time for her to read to him. And then she did it.

"John," she said to me, "I'm going to make it your responsibility to read to Matthew every day. Read him everything you can for as much time as you can."

That was fine with me. For one thing I liked Matthew, at least better than I liked Kate and Anne. Also, since I was oldest, it seemed like a good thing for me to have more responsibility.

The twins are supposed to have done everything faster than I did, walking, talking, tying their shoelaces. Now here was Matthew breaking their records. I liked that. At eighteen months, he already

had a pretty good vocabulary and sometimes spoke in sentences. I thought if I could teach him to read by the time he was three, ol' Kate and Anne would die of shame.

I remember the very first thing I read to Matthew. It was Beatrix Potter's *Tale of Tom Kitten*. Now, Mom had been reading him *Time* magazine and an Agatha Christie novel. When he was really small, she would put him in this little cloth carrier thing and let him ride around with her while she worked. She read to him from a recipe book, circulars that came in the mail, letters from my grandparents, anything.

Well, just about the time she asked me to start reading to him, he had been given a set of those really little books Beatrix Potter wrote, and I figured it would be nice for him to hear a story that made some sense for a change. So I took two or three of them, and Matthew and I went outside to read. I showed him a picture at the start of the Tom Kitten book and began to read. He looked at every picture just as soon as I turned the page, but I couldn't tell if he was enjoying the story. He didn't make a sound.

Well, I finished reading the story, and Matthew slapped his fat little hands onto his fat little knees and said, "Again."

I turned back to the front of the book and read the whole story over again. When I finished, Matthew slapped his knees and nodded his head and said, "Read again."

When the same thing happened over again, I thought maybe this was like the throwing-the-spoon-out-of-the-high-chair trick. You know, when the kid drops his spoon so you can hand it back. Then he drops it again so you will hand it back again. Two things babies love are repetition and getting you to do things for them. I reminded myself that no matter how smart he was, Matthew was still a baby. Anyway, I showed him the other books, which looked like the one we had been reading, and suggested we try *The Tale of Peter Rabbit*.

He said, "Okay," with a big nod and sat there holding his hands on his knees like a little old man.

He leaned forward to study the pictures; just like before he didn't make a sound or move an inch when I started to read. This time though I began to get a funny feeling. When I came to the part about going "lippity—lippity—not very fast," I knew I was reading but I felt it too. I mean I could feel big, strong hindlegs pushing me along in sort of gentle loppety motion. I turned the page. (I could still turn the page and I was still reading the words.) The drawing on the next page was all around us. I know I'm not explaining this right, but how would you explain it? I mean I was reading the book but I knew I was in the book too. I looked at Matthew and just then he wiggled his fat little rabbit body under a wooden fence and I had to crawl under after him and keep reading at the same time. This time he didn't have to ask; we read the book over three—maybe four— times.

When we finally stopped and went back into the house, I didn't believe what had happened. It didn't make sense, so I just didn't believe it. And, of course, Matthew didn't tell anybody. For one thing he didn't think anything strange had happened, although he did tell me I read better stories than Mom. For another thing, even if he had known that stories weren't supposed to come alive like that, he couldn't have explained what had happened. He had a good vocabulary but not that good.

For part of every day I took Matthew outside to read to him. After a while I stopped not believing and began to understand that reading to Matthew was not like any other reading I had ever done. I thought maybe there was something really strange about that set of Beatrix Potter books.

We read the whole set. I knew just what it felt like to be in a hole underground with Mrs. Tittlemouse, how Mr. Jackson's toothless toad mouth looked, how beeswax smelled, and what honeydew tasted like. I got to know all the sights, sounds, smells, and tastes of Thomasina Tittlemouse's house because she was one of Matthew's favorites.

We only read *The Story of a Fierce Bad Rabbit* once.
Being shot at was too scary.

Sometimes, Mrs. Holt, the lady who stayed with
us during the day, would be in our kitchen ironing.
And Matthew and I would go outside and read about
Mrs. Tiggy-Winkle, who would also be ironing. The
smell of the hot iron on the damp clothes was just
the same—inside the house and inside the story.

I don't know how my mother finally came to
notice that I wasn't reading anything but Beatrix
Potter, but toward the end of the summer she told
me I'd either have to start reading other things or
she'd put the twins in charge of Matthew's reading.
She said if I just stuck with "those tiny books"
because I resented reading to the baby I should
say so.

I told her I was reading those books because they were what Matthew liked, and Matthew jumped in and said, "They's Matthew's best stories."

"You see, you're stunting his vocabulary. He isn't talking any better than he was two months ago."

"Don't you be silly, you silly old mom," Matthew told her in Mrs. McGregor's words from a book about the flopsy bunnies.

"He doesn't mean to be calling you silly," I said quickly. "He's just showing you some words he has learned."

"I don't think I like the words he has been learning." She was studying his face. She pulled her eyes away, and said firmly to me, "Start on *Winnie-the-Pooh* tomorrow."

"Sure," I agreed. "I'll get out the Pooh books tonight."

We must have spent two or three weeks reading *Winnie-the-Pooh*. At first it was just like reading had always been—before I began reading to Matthew. Then one day, after we'd finished reading, Matthew asked me which stick I thought really won in the Poohsticks game.

"Well, Piglet's was the crooked one."

And then it hit me. I was seeing the game, picturing it the way I had watched it happen. I focused on the stream in my memory and counted the sticks as they appeared out of the shadow of the bridge. There were two extra sticks: Matthew and I had been in the game. The Pooh stories were different from the Beatrix Potter ones. We never got into the Five Hundred Acre Wood while we were reading, but after we put the book aside we could "remember" things as though they'd happened to us.

Over the next year we read some books that came to life and some that didn't. You really get into some stories but some are just there to be read.

During the school year, I didn't read to Matthew so often. By the time he was four, Matthew could read simple books for himself.

Sometimes he'd bring me a picture book, and say, "Read, John."

"Matthew," I'd say, "it's mostly just pictures. You read it."

The book would hang at his side and he'd shake his head.

"It's not the same, John. It doesn't read for Matthew."

When Matthew was five or six, I got interested in pirates and was reading *Treasure Island*. He kept pestering me to read, so to keep him quiet I started reading my book out loud to him. I didn't go back to the beginning and start over for him. I just picked up right where I was and read from there.

I had been letting this kid *beg* me to read to him? I soon realized I ought to be paying him to listen to me read. *Treasure Island* had been a good book before; suddenly it was great.

I hadn't read a full page out loud before I found myself inside an apple barrel. Sure, I could see the page in front of me and I was still reading, but I

could also see the rough staves of the apple barrel. I could hear Jim Hawkins breathing beside me, and I could feel Matthew's hand on my arm. All around us was a smell like apple cider. Just beyond us, on the other side of the barrel, was Long John Silver, his voice deep and honeyed-sounding.

Once in a while when we were going to read, Kate and Anne would sit beside us saying "Read to us, too."

"No," Matthew would say, "you go away."

"We want to listen too," Anne would wail.

"No, John reads to Matthew," Matthew would tell them.

While we couldn't get "into" some books no matter how hard we tried, in others a whole world would open up. The place, the characters, everything that happened would be real.

And all the time we were reading, Matthew was growing up. I was never sure how much he understood of the novels I liked to read now, but when you're living the story what difference do a few five-syllable words make?

By the time Matthew was seven and I was fourteen, we were both reading different sorts of books on our own. And still, books only became real for me when I was reading out loud to Matthew. I suspected that was also the only time the magic worked for him too. So, of course, I found time to read to him.

From the very start, *The Call of the Wild* was a funny book. What I mean is that it drew us into it in strange ways. Sometimes I could feel the warmth of a parka around me and could feel myself sliding over the packed, frozen snow at the back of a sled. At

other times as I read I could feel my feet striking the crusted snow and the straps of a harness biting into my shoulders as I raced along as part of the team pulling the sled. I never knew who I'd be or where I'd be in the story.

We'd gotten about two-thirds of the way through the book when Matthew was hit by a ball and ended up unconscious in the hospital.

At first, Anne and Kate and I weren't allowed to see him. Even when they told us he wasn't going to die, only the adults could go in.

"He's okay though, isn't he, Mom?" Kate asked.

Mom just started to cry. Finally, my dad said, "He doesn't know us. He's fine, except that he doesn't know us. He doesn't know anything."

"Amnesia?" Anne said wonderingly.

"Unconscious" isn't amnesia, but I knew how she felt. I mean stuff like that doesn't *really* happen.

"The doctors say it may take time," Dad said.

"Or it may take forever," my mom added angrily. "It's as though it's Matthew but not Matthew." She was crying again.

Later that day, we three kids got to see Matthew, but only just see him. We weren't allowed to stay at all.

A week later he was still in the hospital and nothing had changed. The doctors said that there was no reason he shouldn't recover but that head injuries are strange things.

"I know he'll be all right," Mom said that evening. "It's just as though his mind were wandering off in some other realm."

I fell asleep that night thinking of what she'd said, imagining Matthew's body here and his mind somewhere else. All that night I had crazy dreams. Time after time I could see Matthew just ahead of me. I'd almost reach him and then he'd slip away. In one dream we were rabbits, and then we were boys tumbling past the roots of a tree into the ground. In a later dream that same night I chased Matthew through foggy London streets. Then, dodging pirates on a sandy beach, I looked for Matthew on an island.

I woke up the next morning determined to get Matthew back. If he was lost somewhere outside himself, I meant to find him.

"I want to visit Matthew," I said at breakfast. "I want to go and read to him."

Everybody objected. They argued that you can't read to somebody who's unconscious.

I didn't argue. I just kept saying, "I want to go read to Matthew."

And finally they agreed. I didn't care that it was a schoolday, but my parents did. They said I could go to the hospital as soon as school was over. I had to accept that, but I didn't think about anything else all day.

When school was over, my dad picked me up and drove me to the hospital. I asked him to leave me there.

"I'll be back around six," he told me.

Beside Matthew's bed, I took a long look at my brother. He was a round-faced little kid, but not pudgy like he'd been as a baby. I watched the short fingers of his hand lying on the sheet. I was really seeing him. He had always just been my "brother," the baby-faced kid I read to.

A clear picture came to me of an afternoon we'd spent—me and Matthew, Alan Breck and David

Balfour—in the hollowed-out top of a tall rock. There'd been soldiers swarming all around on the ground below our rock searching for us. It was as much as our lives were worth for anyone to realize that we were there, the four of us, right above them.

Matthew had gripped my arm and said, "He'll get us out safe, won't he? Alan Breck would never let the soldiers catch us."

He'd called him "Ah-lan," broadening the "a"
and rolling the name just the way Alan himself would
say it and his eyes had shone with hero worship. I
hadn't felt jealous then, but I guess I did standing
beside the hospital bed. I needed to be as big a hero
as Alan Breck in *Kidnapped,* bigger really, because
Alan Breck was a showoff. He'd get you into trouble
and then pull you out so you'd be grateful and
admire him for it. Still, I wished he was here now.

I pulled a chair right up to the head of the bed
and opened the copy of *The Call of the Wild* that I'd
brought with me.

Just the day before he'd been hit by that ball Matthew had been with me in the frozen northland. I didn't know where he might be now, but this was the only way I knew how to search for him.

I began to read, "Late next morning Buck led the long team up the street. There was nothing lively about it, no snap or go in him and his fellows. They were starting dead weary."

I read three full pages and all that happened was that I was mouthing words from the printed page. Nothing I'd ever read alone had come to life for me. I needed Matthew and he wasn't there.

My mother had cried for the first few days after Matthew was hit. Kate and Anne had cried loudly and wetly that first night. I hadn't cried. But now sitting there reading out loud to a kid who couldn't hear me, I felt my eyes get wet. I wouldn't let a tear fall. I just kept reading. Pretty soon my nose started running, and I had to keep wiping it on my hand.

Then I started reading and talking to Matthew at the same time. I was saying, "I know you're here, Matthew. Come on, let me see you." Then I would read another line or two just to keep the story moving. Then I'd say, "I need to find you, Matthew.

We've got to stay together. We're in this together. I'm here with you." And then I'd read some more.

I don't know when I began to feel the drop in the temperature, but that was the first change. I was cold. I kept talking and I kept reading.

The wind seemed to be hitting my face at gale-force so I had trouble keeping my eyes open. Still I kept reading. Snow seemed to be sticking in my hair—no, my fur, the fur that covered me. I gulped a deep, relieved breath of icy air. I was in the story. I read of the dogs racing over the ice, and I felt my feet, my *four* feet, striking the hard, cold surface.

Just in front of me I could see the big, powerful haunches of a Saint Bernard, and I knew I was right behind Buck, who was leading the team.

"Matthew!" I inserted the cry into the printed text and tried to look around me. I didn't have far to look. My teammate, the sled dog harnessed in beside me, was short with powerful legs and such a fluffy, fuzzy coat that it looked like puppy fur. I recognized my brother in a single glance.

I choked on a laugh and kept reading and running.

After a few pages of icy racing, the team was pulling to a halt and unhitched. Night was falling when someone threw us meat. I dug a hole below the snow and Matthew and I curled up in shared warmth. Night lasted less than the space of a paragraph, but it was a night just the same.

How am I going to get us out of here? I wondered. Always before just to stop reading had been enough, but to stop reading now might take me out of the story leaving Matthew behind. I had found him, and I wasn't going to lose him again.

What if I was doing the wrong thing? Maybe I was pushing Matthew beyond his own physical limits. The animals were so underfed and overworked that the entire team was near exhaustion. And things were growing steadily worse.

Just about then, John Thornton appeared in the story—a hero, at least a hero for Buck.

"If you strike that dog again, I'll kill you," I said, speaking John Thornton's words.

As always I could see the printed page in front of me even as I felt ice forming on my fur. I forced myself to look ahead in the story.

Halfway down the page my eyes caught the words that spelled disaster. Within the next few lines John Thornton would separate Buck from his cruel master, and a line or two after that the whole team, all the dogs except Buck, would go hurtling to their deaths when the icy bottom of the trail dropped out.

I had already been mixing my own words with those of the story. I decided to try it again.

"I'm John Thornton," I said out loud, adding the assertion to the story. "My name is John Thornton," I repeated.

I could see Buck stretched out on the snow where the man called Hal had been thrashing him, and my view of him seemed changed from the moment before. The team was changed too. The dogs were harnessed in single file. Behind Buck there was now only one sled dog, the fuzzy, half-grown pup I'd recognized as Matthew. Where was I?

Struggling to get my bearings, I read on. Hal drew his long hunting knife. And, as I saw it, I knew he meant to kill the man who stood between him and the dog he had been beating. He meant to kill John. His hatred was so strong I could feel it, almost even see it like hot breath in cold air. As it touched me, I knew it was hatred toward me.

I am John, I thought. Of course, it's me he wants to kill.

I brought my hand down hard across his knuckles, knocking the knife to the ground. Then I added

something else to the story, saying the words out loud, acting and describing the action at the same time.

"John picked up the knife and with two strokes cut Buck's traces, and then with two more swift strokes severed the traces of the fuzzy, young sled dog behind Buck . . . Hal had no fight left in him." I picked up the story and continued it just the way Jack London wrote it. Only this time a stocky young

sled dog had joined John and Buck to watch in safety as the people and the team disappeared through the ice a quarter of a mile down the trail.

And this time when John Thornton reached out saying "You poor devil," he reached with both hands and met the fur of *two* half-frozen dogs.

I felt the thick fur of the young dog's neck beneath my fingers. Relief made me weak. The sled dog that was Matthew was safe, but again I wondered if I had been a fool to try to reach my brother this way. I had found him, even touched him, somewhere out there in the no-man's-land of Jack London's Alaska. I hoped it hadn't done any harm.

The reunion between Buck and John Thornton was followed right away by the destruction of the sled and that ended the chapter. I knew I'd have to go on, but just for the moment I stopped, wondering what other traps might lie ahead of us.

Slowly I closed the book, holding my place with my finger, and then I closed my eyes. I had to wipe my nose again.

"John?"

I opened my eyes and looked around in disbelief. Matthew had raised his head and was looking at me, clear-eyed and knowing.

"Aren't you going to read any more of it, John?"